By George R. R. Martin

A Song of Ice and Fire

Book One: A Game of Thrones
Book Two: A Clash of Kings
Book Three: A Storm of Swords
Book Four: A Feast for Crows
Book Five: A Dance with Dragons

Dying of the Light
Windhaven (with Lisa Tuttle)
Fevre Dream
The Armageddon Rag
Dead Man's Hand (with John J. Miller)

Short Story Collections

Dreamsongs: Volume I
Dreamsongs: Volume II
A Song for Lya and Other Stories
Songs of Stars and Shadows
Sandkings
Songs the Dead Men Sing
Nightflyers
Tuf Voyaging
Portraits of His Children
Quartet

Edited by George R. R. Martin

New Voices in Science Fiction, Volumes 1–4
The Science Fiction Weight Loss Book (with Isaac Asimov and
Martin Harry Greenberg)
The John W. Campbell Awards, Volume 5
Night Visions 3
Wild Cards I–XXI
Old Mars (with Gardner Dozois)

The Wit and Wisdom of
Tyrion Lannister

The Wit and Wisdom of
Tyrion Lannister

George R. R. Martin

Illustrated by Jonty Clarke

Bantam Books
New York

Published in the United States by Bantam Books, an imprint of The Random House Publishing Group, a division of Random House LLC, a Penguin Random House Company, New York.

BANTAM BOOKS and the HOUSE colophon are registered trademarks of Random House LLC.

ISBN 978-0-345-53912-0
eBook ISBN 978-0-345-53914-4

Printed in the United States of America on acid-free paper

www.bantamdell.com

57986

Interior design by Foltz Design

The Wit and Wisdom of
Tyrion Lannister

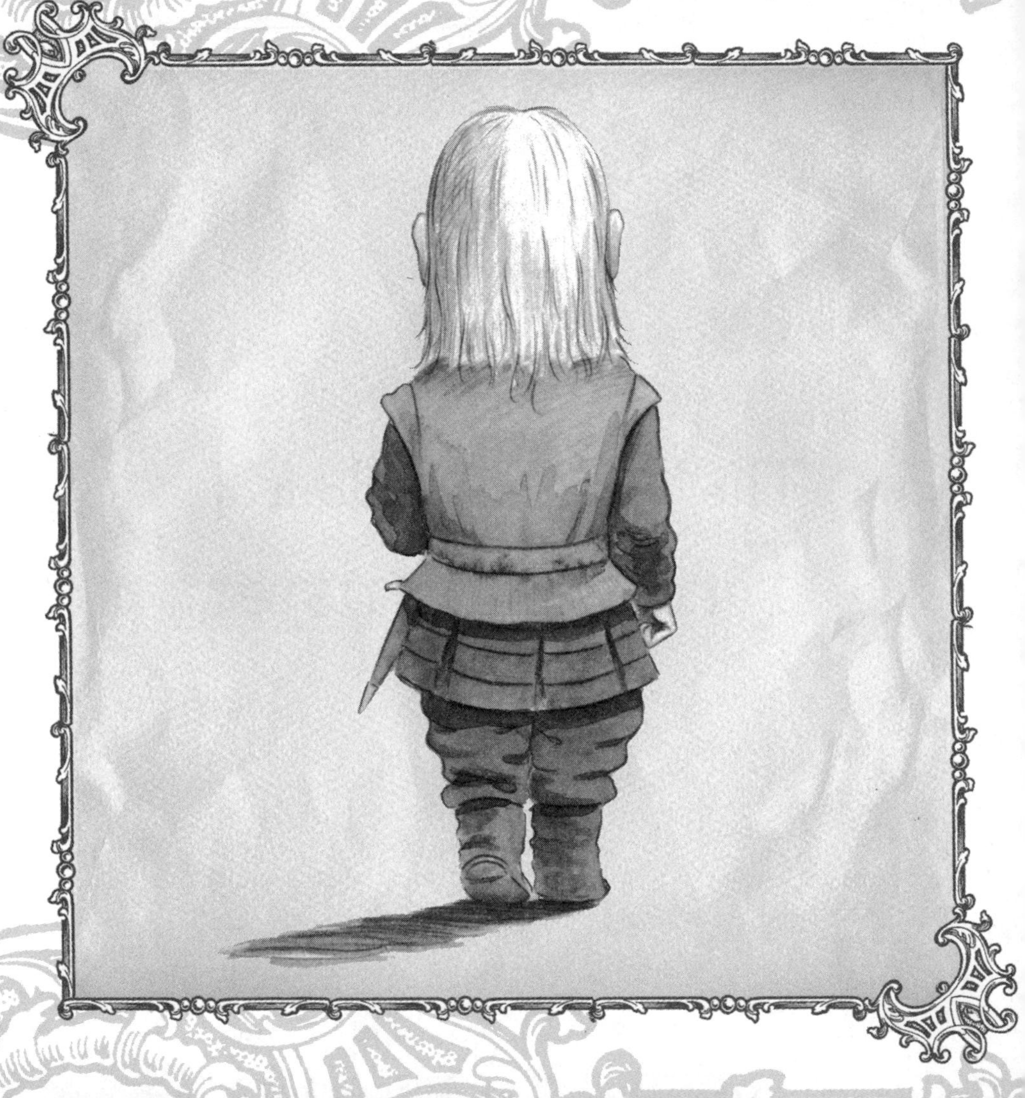

On Being a Dwarf

All dwarfs are bastards in their father's eyes.

—*A Game of Thrones*

What joy to be a dwarf.

—*A Dance with Dragons*

I was born. I lived. I am guilty of being a dwarf, I confess it. And no matter how many times my good father forgave me, I have persisted in my infamy.

—*A Storm of Swords*

Whatever you wear, you're still a dwarf. You'll never be as tall as that knight on the steps, him with his long straight legs and hard stomach and wide manly shoulders.

—*A Storm of Swords*

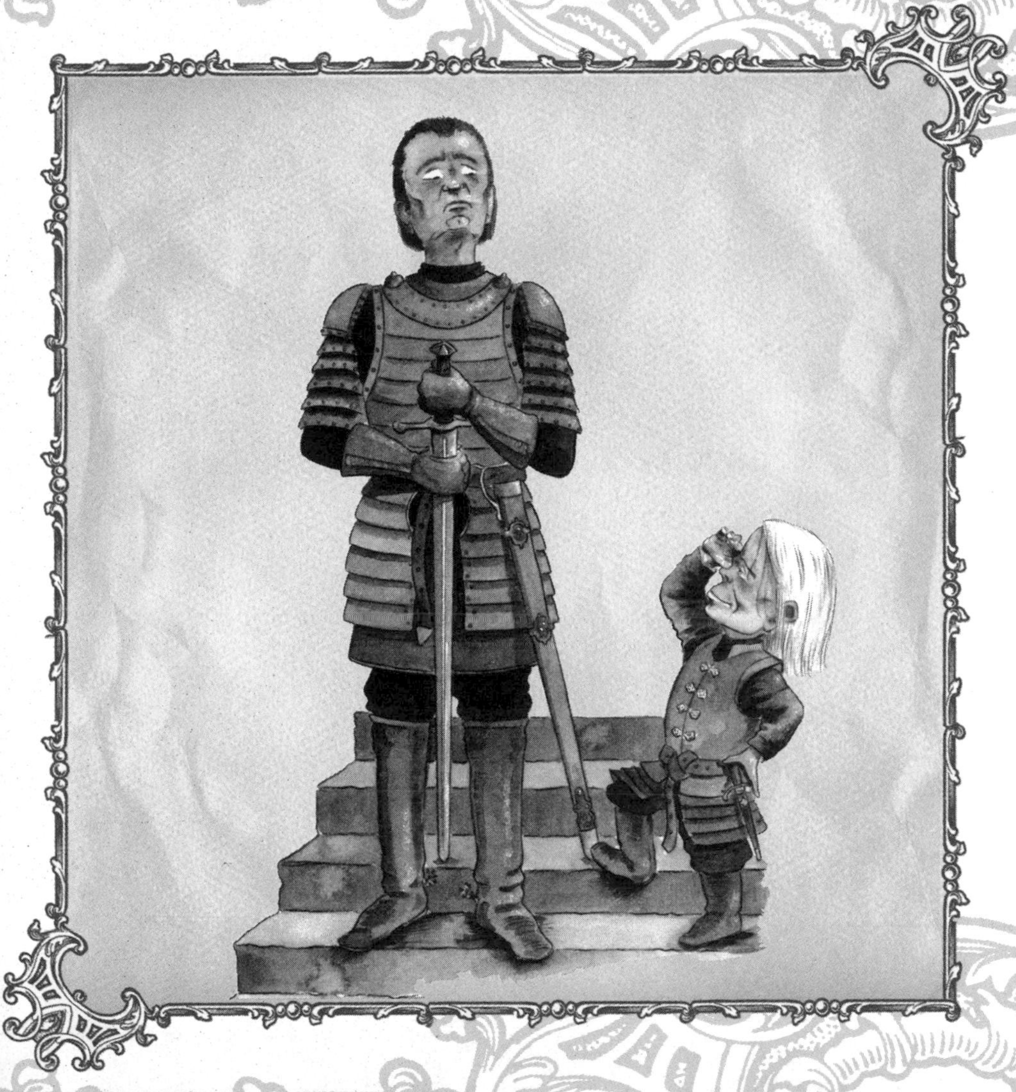

I have been called many things,
but giant is seldom one of them.

—*A Game of Thrones*

The only thing more pitiful than a dwarf without a nose is a dwarf without a nose who has no gold.

—*A Dance with Dragons*

Pissing is the least of my talents.
You ought to see me shit.

—A Dance with Dragons

No one fears a dwarf.

—A Dance with Dragons

All dwarfs may be bastards,
yet not all bastards need be dwarfs.

—*A Game of Thrones*

I'm short, not blind.

—*A Clash of Kings*

Do you think I might stand taller in black?

—*A Dance with Dragons*

I am malformed, scarred, and small, but . . .
abed, when the candles are blown out,
I am made no worse than other men.
In the dark, I am the Knight of Flowers.

—*A Storm of Swords*

Dwarfs are a jape of the gods,
but men make eunuchs.

—*A Clash of Kings*

They say I'm half a man.
What does that make the lot of you?

—*A Clash of Kings*

I have a tender spot in my heart for cripples
and bastards and broken things.

—*A Game of Thrones*

The gods must have been drunk
when they got to me.

—*A Dance with Dragons*

I only need half my wits to be a match for you.

—*A Dance with Dragons*

I had dreamt enough for one small life.
And of such follies: love, justice, friendship,
glory. As well dream of being tall.

—*A Dance with Dragons*

It may be good luck to rub the head of a dwarf, but it is even better luck to suck on a dwarf's cock.

—*A Dance with Dragons*

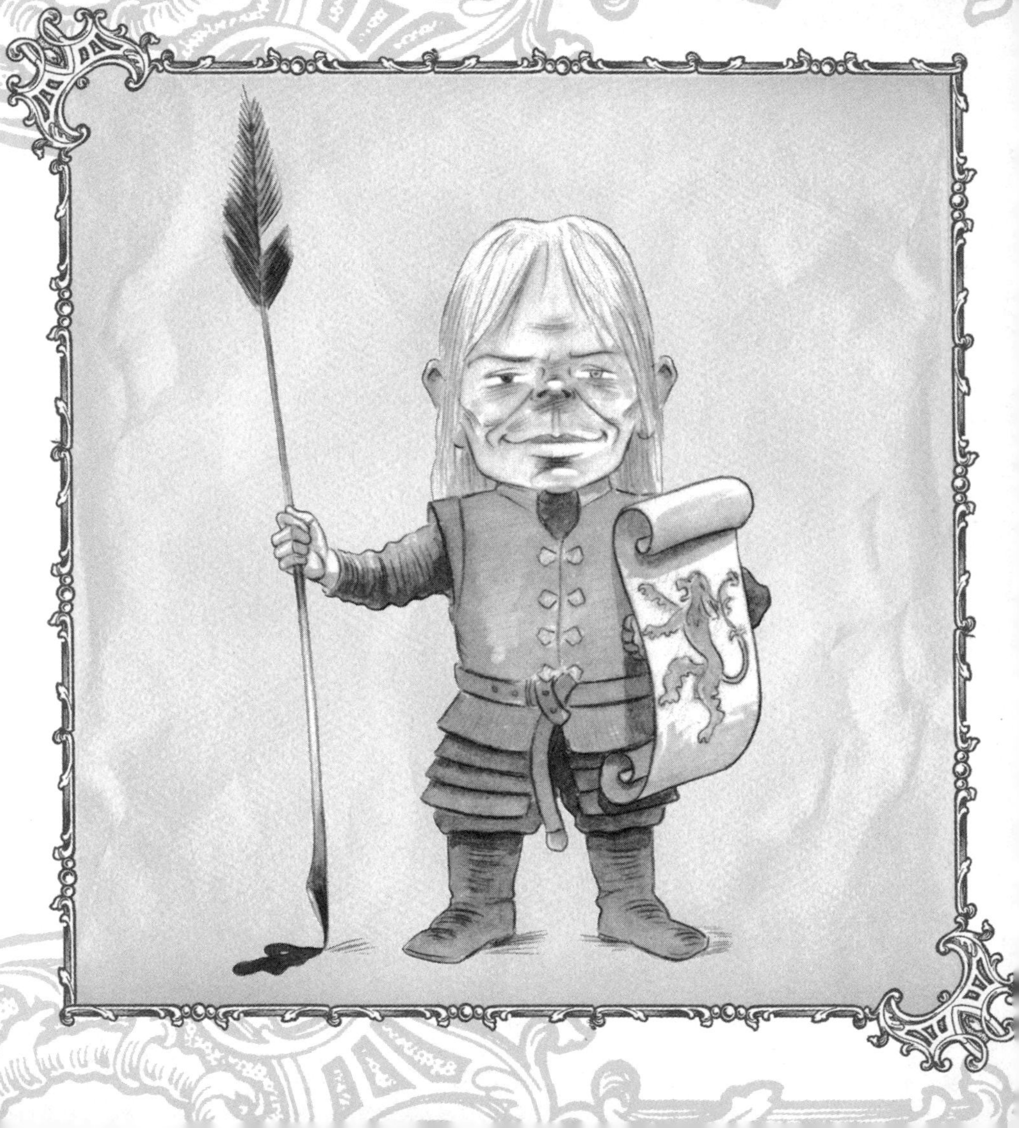

On the Power of Words

My mind is my weapon. My brother has his sword, King Robert has his warhammer, and I have my mind . . . and a mind needs books as a sword needs a whetstone if it is to keep its edge.

—*A Game of Thrones*

Duck has his sword, I my quill and parchment.

—*A Dance with Dragons*

When you tear out a man's tongue, you are not proving him a liar, you're only telling the world that you fear what he might say.

—*A Clash of Kings*

Sleep is good. And books are better.

—*A Clash of Kings*

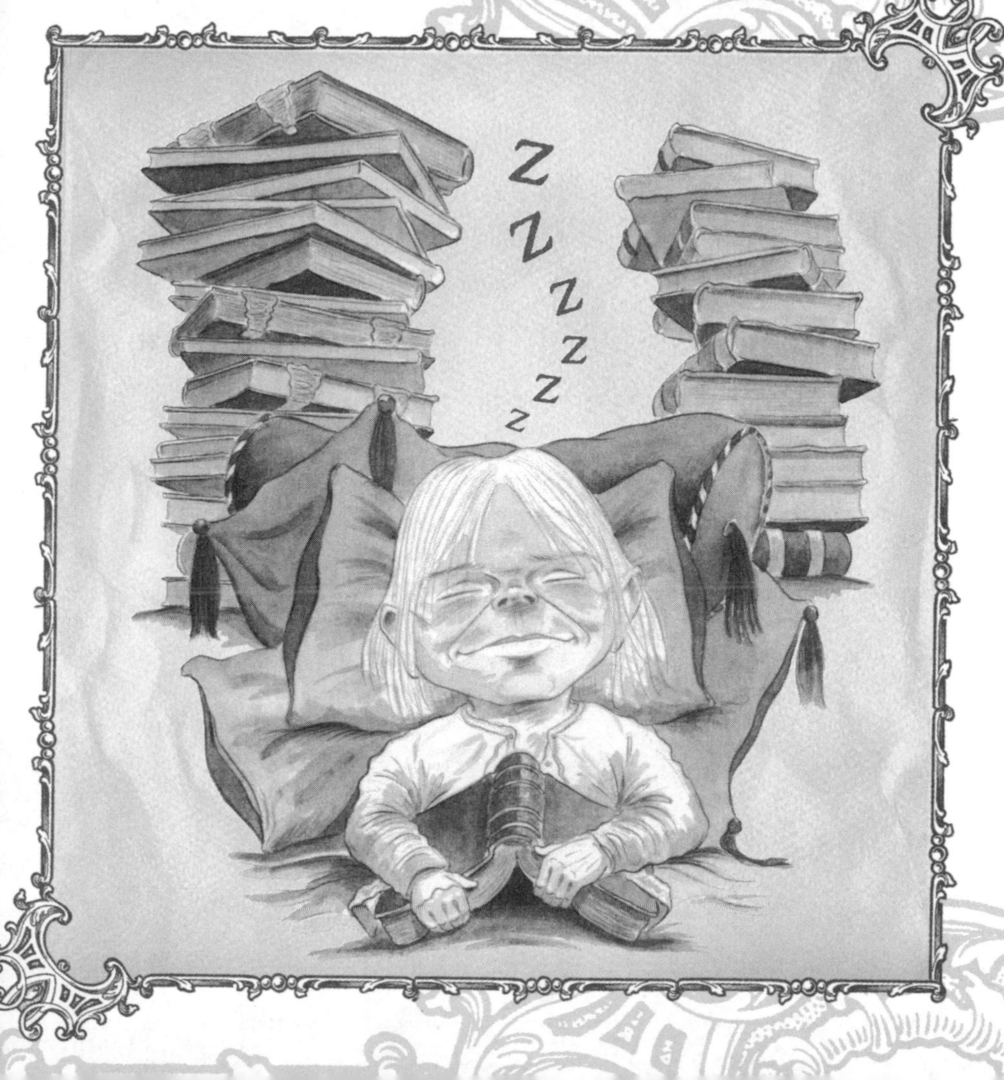
Z Z Z Z Z Z

Let them see that their words can cut you, and you'll never be free of the mockery. If they want to give you a name, take it, make it your own. Then they can't hurt you with it anymore.

—*A Game of Thrones*

Guard your tongue before it digs your grave.

—*A Storm of Swords*

Words are wind.

—*A Dance with Dragons*

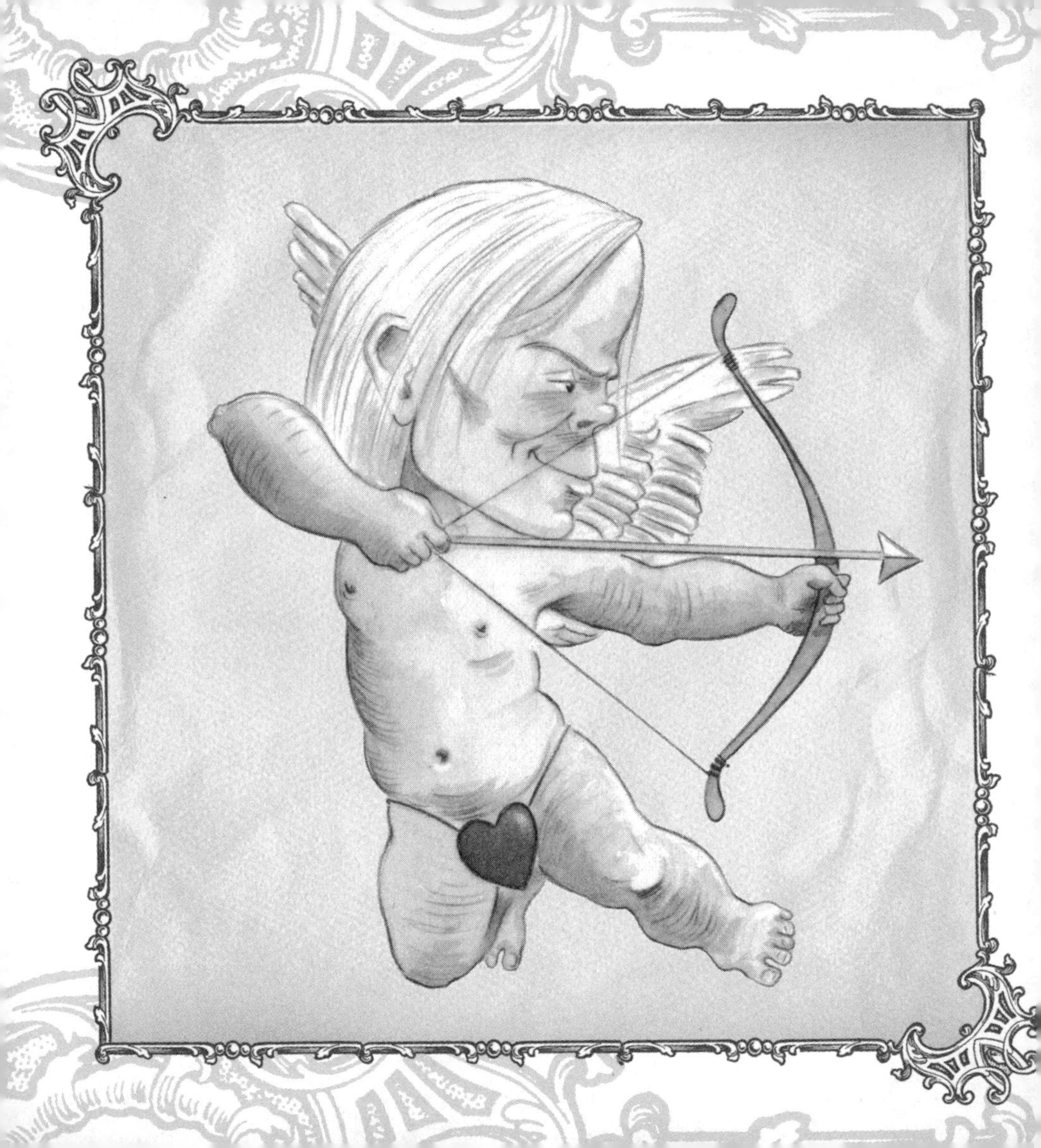

On Romance

Shy maids are my favorite sort.
Aside from wanton ones . . . but sometimes
the ugliest ones are the hungriest once abed.

—*A Dance with Dragons*

My own father could not love me.
Why would you if not for gold?

—*A Dance with Dragons*

A man grows weary of having no lovers
but his fingers.

—*A Dance with Dragons*

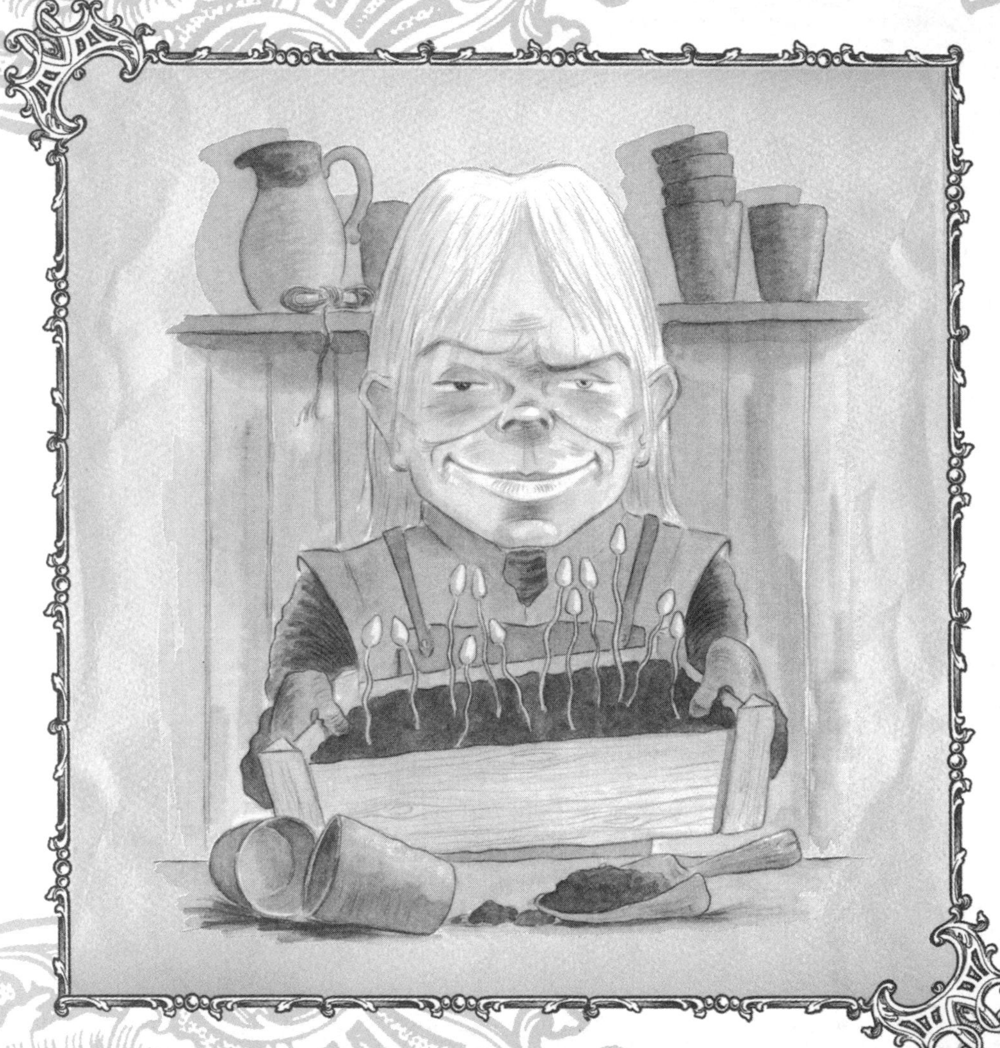

I plant my little seeds just as often as I can.

—*A Storm of Swords*

With whores, the young ones smell much better, but the old ones know more tricks.

—*A Dance with Dragons*

I would prefer a whore who is reasonably young, with as pretty a face as you can find. If she has washed sometime this year, I shall be glad. If she hasn't, wash her.

—*A Game of Thrones*

Sleep with Lollys? I'd sooner cut it off
and feed it to the goats.

—*A Storm of Swords*

Your Grace, if you take my tongue,
you will leave me no way at all to pleasure
this sweet wife you gave me.

—*A Storm of Swords*

A dwarf's cock has magical powers.

—*A Dance with Dragons*

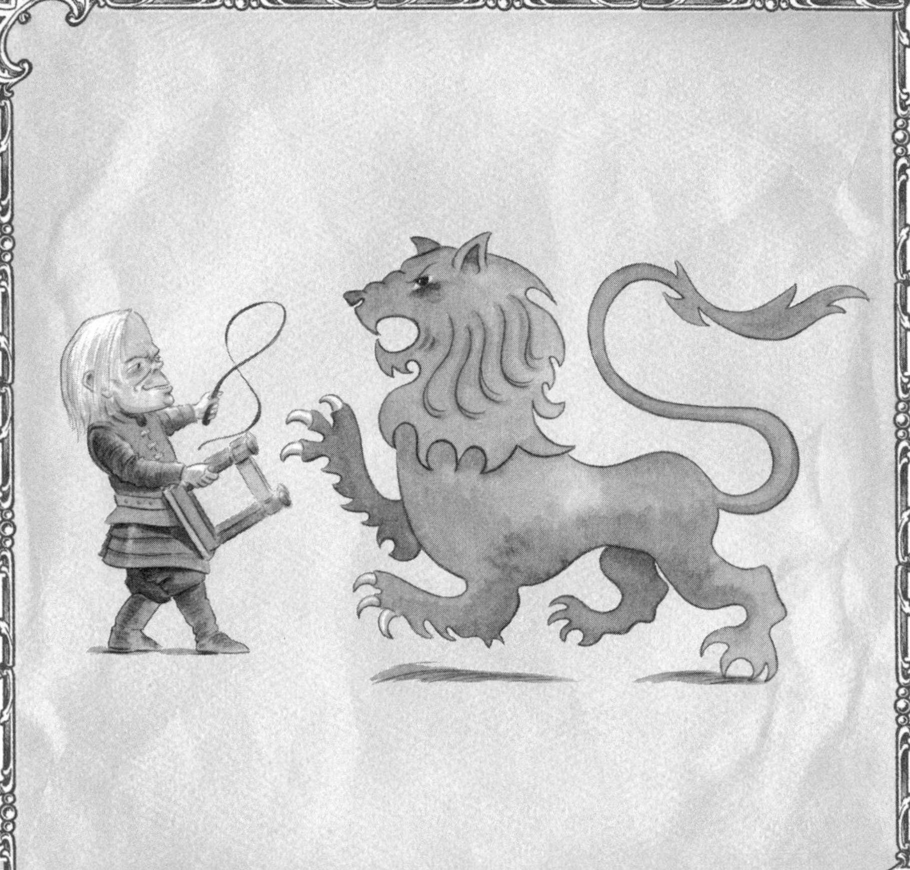

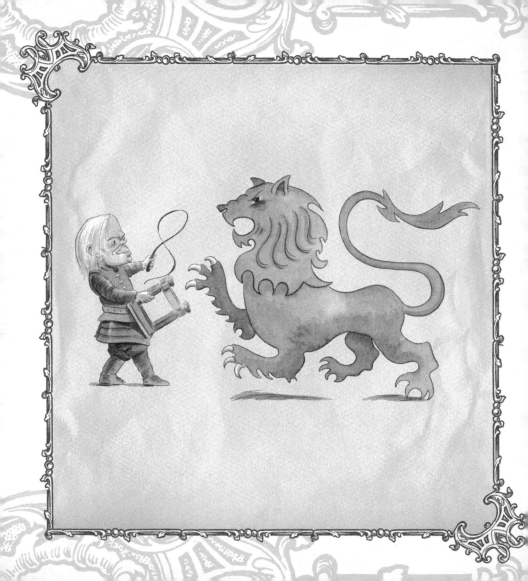

On Family Values

A Lannister always pays his debts.

—*A Game of Thrones*

I *never* bet against my family.

—*A Game of Thrones*

Hard hands and no sense of humor
makes for a bad marriage.

—*A Dance with Dragons*

I should say something, but what?
Pardon me, Father, but it's our brother
she wants to marry.

—*A Storm of Swords*

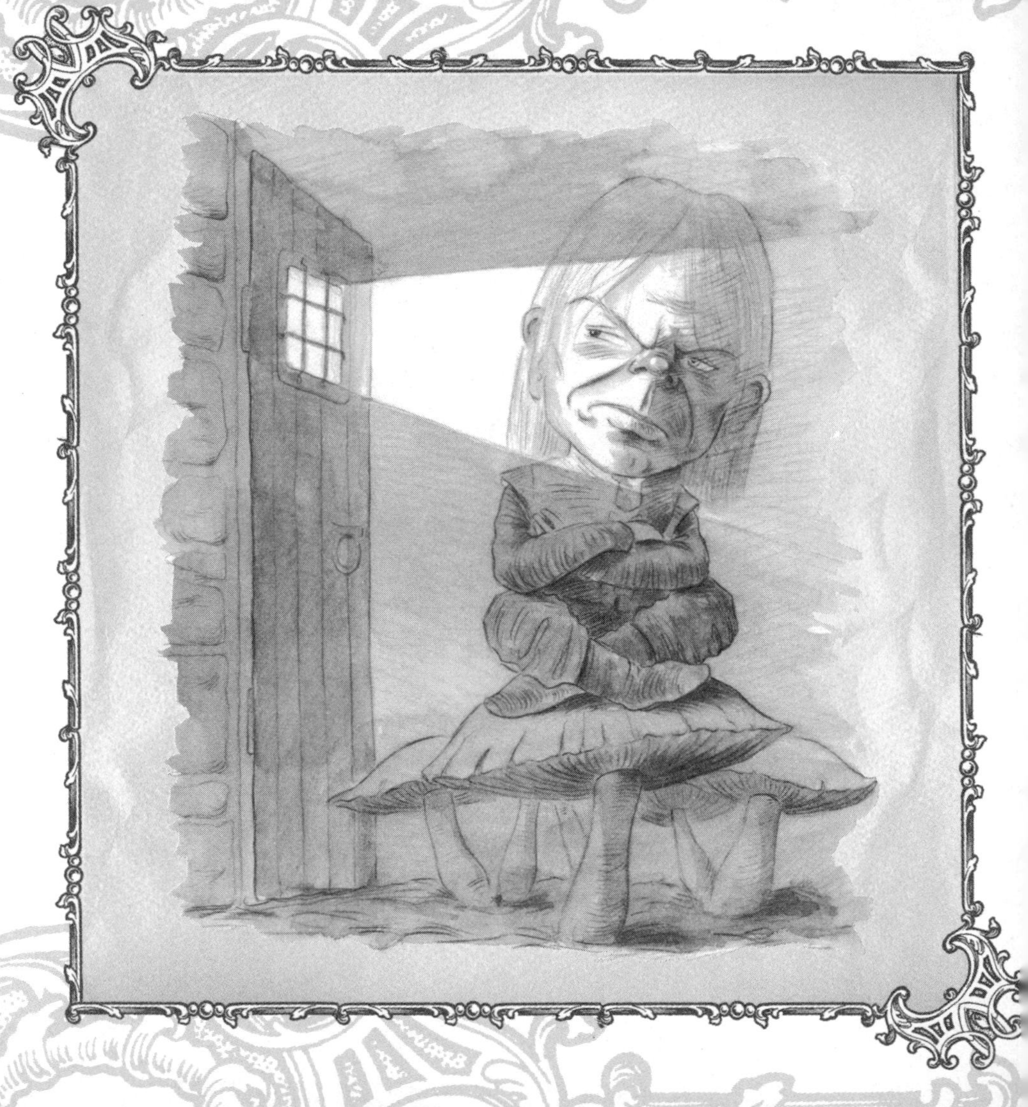

My sister has mistaken me for a mushroom.
She keeps me in the dark and feeds me shit.

—*A Storm of Swords*

Kinslaying is dry work.
It gives a man a thirst.

—*A Dance with Dragons*

Have no fear, I won't kill you,
you are no kin of mine.

—*A Dance with Dragons*

The man who kills his own blood is cursed forever in the sight of gods and men.

—*A Clash of Kings*

I learned long ago that it is considered
rude to vomit on your brother.

—*A Game of Thrones*

Kinslaying was not enough, I needed
a cunt and wine to seal my ruin.

—*A Dance with Dragons*

I have never liked you, Cersei, but you were my own sister, so I never did you harm. You've ended that. I will hurt you for this. I don't know how yet, but give me time. A day will come when you think you are safe and happy, and suddenly your joy will turn to ashes in your mouth, and you'll know the debt is paid.

—*A Clash of Kings*

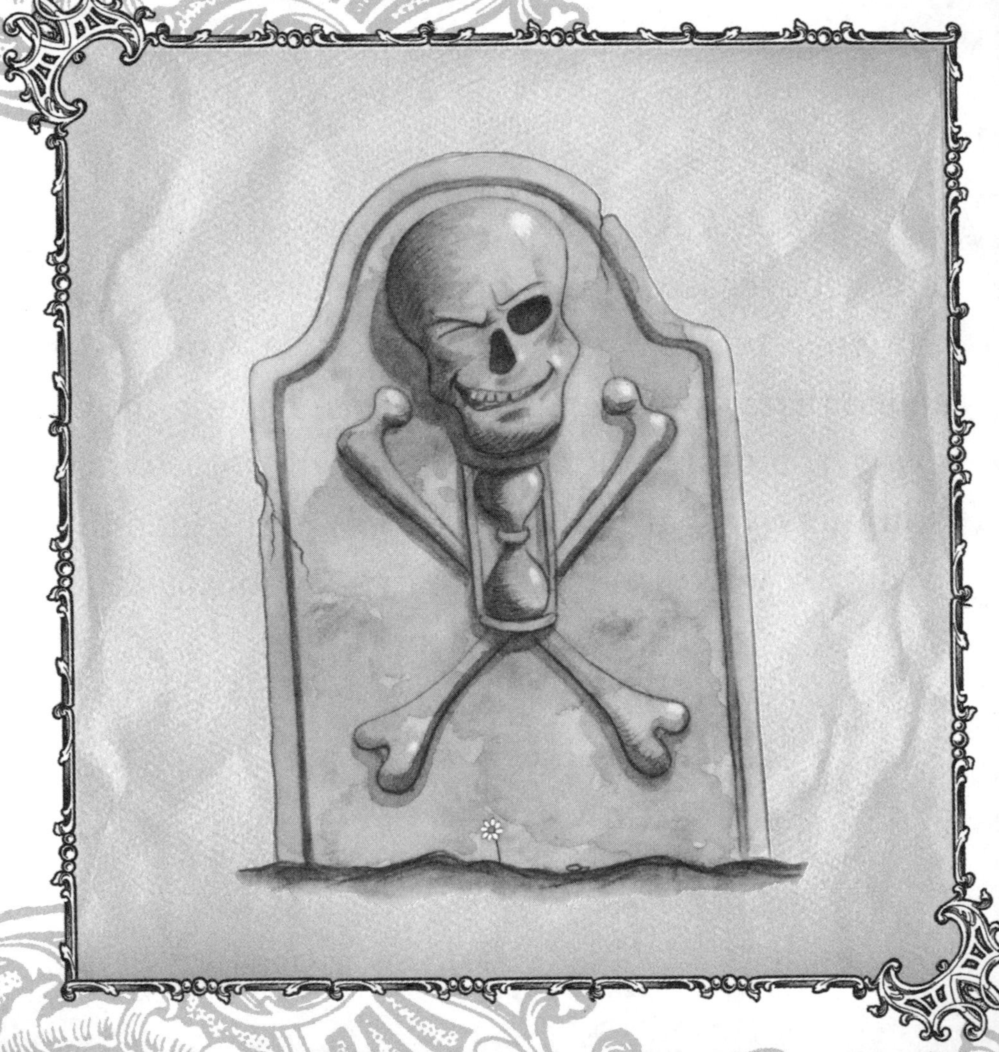

On the Human Condition

The gods are blind.
And men see only what they wish.

—*A Dance with Dragons*

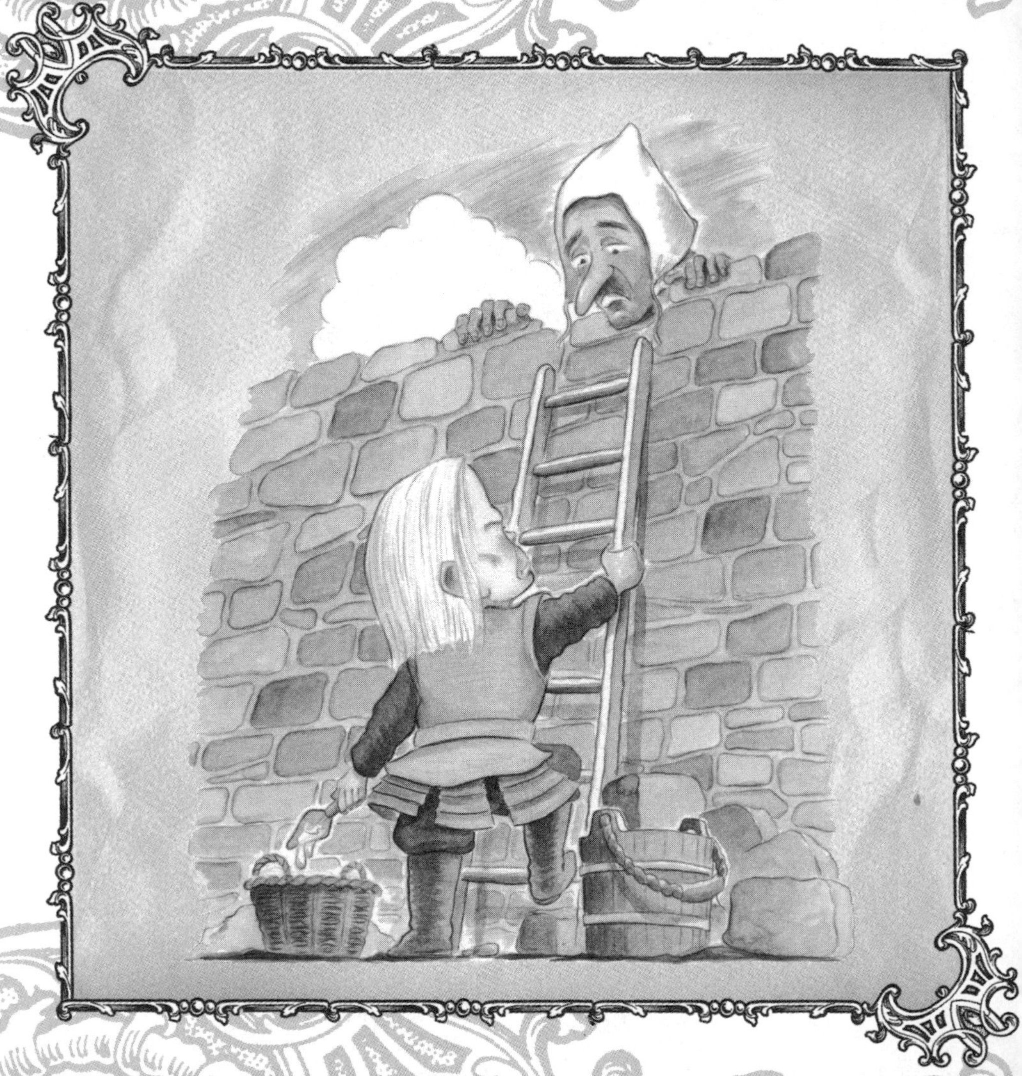

Why is it that when one man builds a wall, the next man immediately needs to know what's on the other side?

—*A Game of Thrones*

I think life is a jape.
Yours, mine, everyone's.

—*A Dance with Dragons*

There has never been a slave who did not choose to be a slave. Their choice may be between bondage and death, but the choice is always there.

—*A Dance with Dragons*

Death is so terribly final,
while life is full of possibilities.

—*A Game of Thrones*

An honest kiss, a little kindness, everyone deserves that much, however big or small.

—*A Dance with Dragons*

Every fool loves to hear that he's important.

—*A Dance with Dragons*

Never forget who you are, for surely the world will not. Make it your strength. Then it can never be your weakness. Armor yourself in it, and it will never be used to hurt you.

—*A Game of Thrones*

A little honest loathing might be refreshing,
like a tart wine after too much sweet.

—*A Dance with Dragons*

We all need to be mocked from time to time,
lest we start to take ourselves too seriously.

—*A Game of Thrones*

Men are such faithless creatures.

—*A Clash of Kings*

Age makes ruins of us all.

—*A Dance with Dragons*

We are all going to die.

—*A Dance with Dragons*

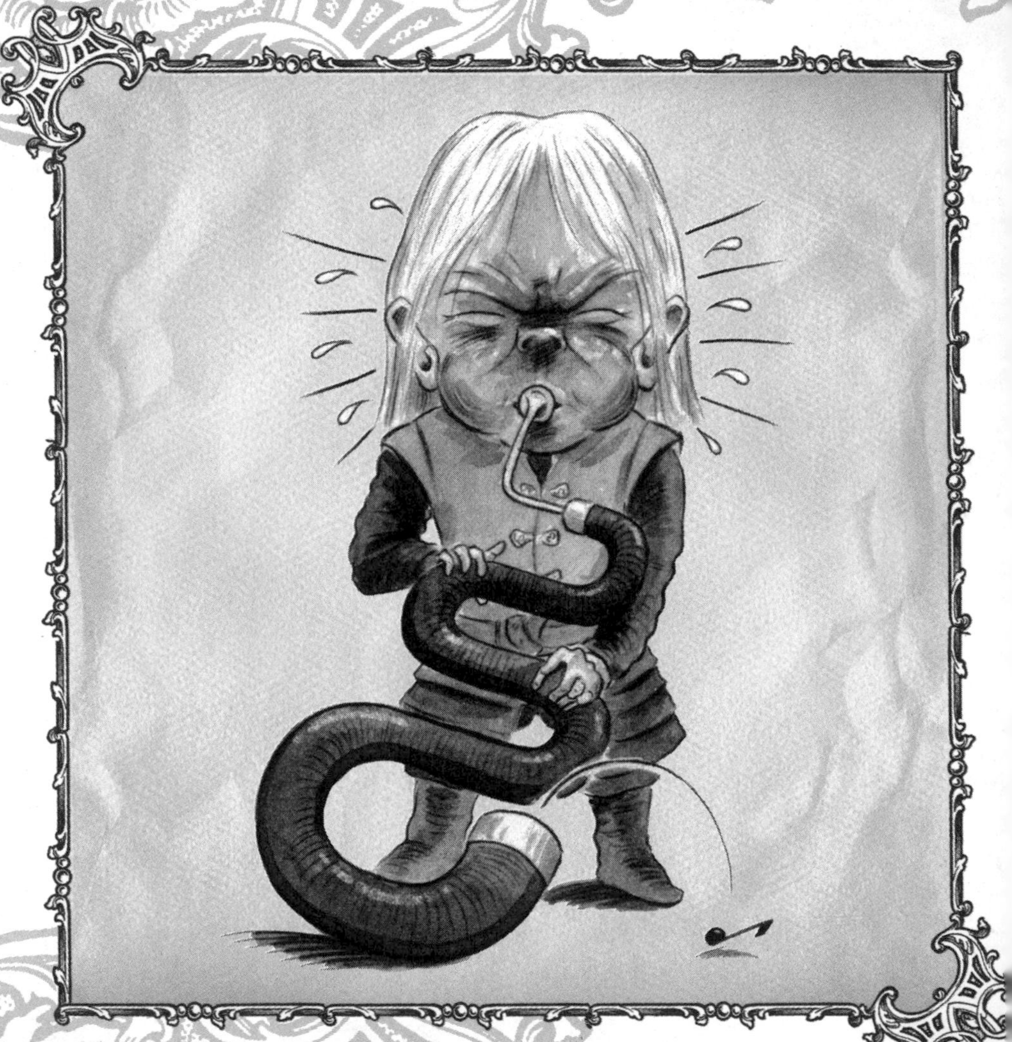

On Music

Never believe anything you hear in a song.

—*A Storm of Swords*

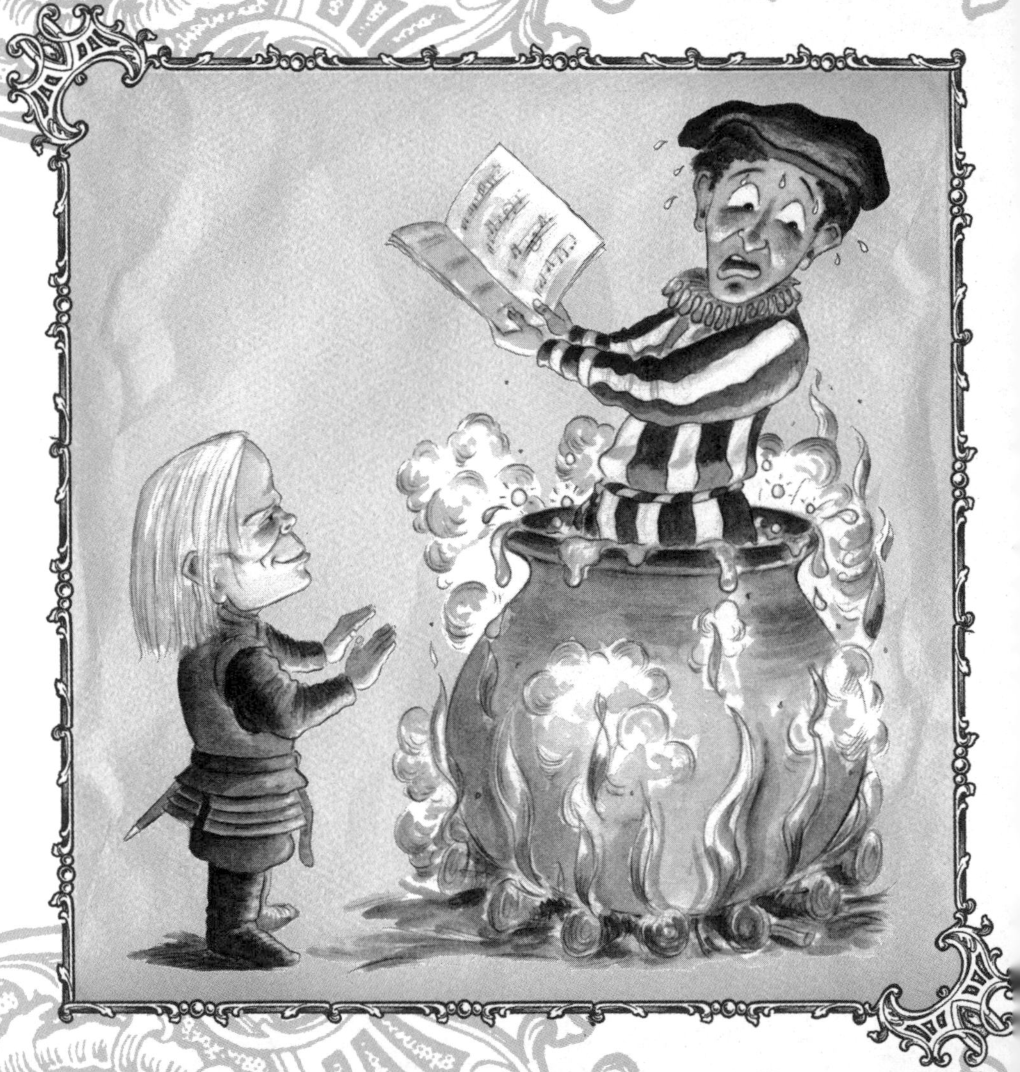

I have killed mothers, fathers, nephews, lovers, men and women, kings and whores. A singer once annoyed me, so I had the bastard stewed.

—*A Dance with Dragons*

If I am ever Hand again, the first thing
I'll do is hang all the singers.

—*A Storm of Swords*

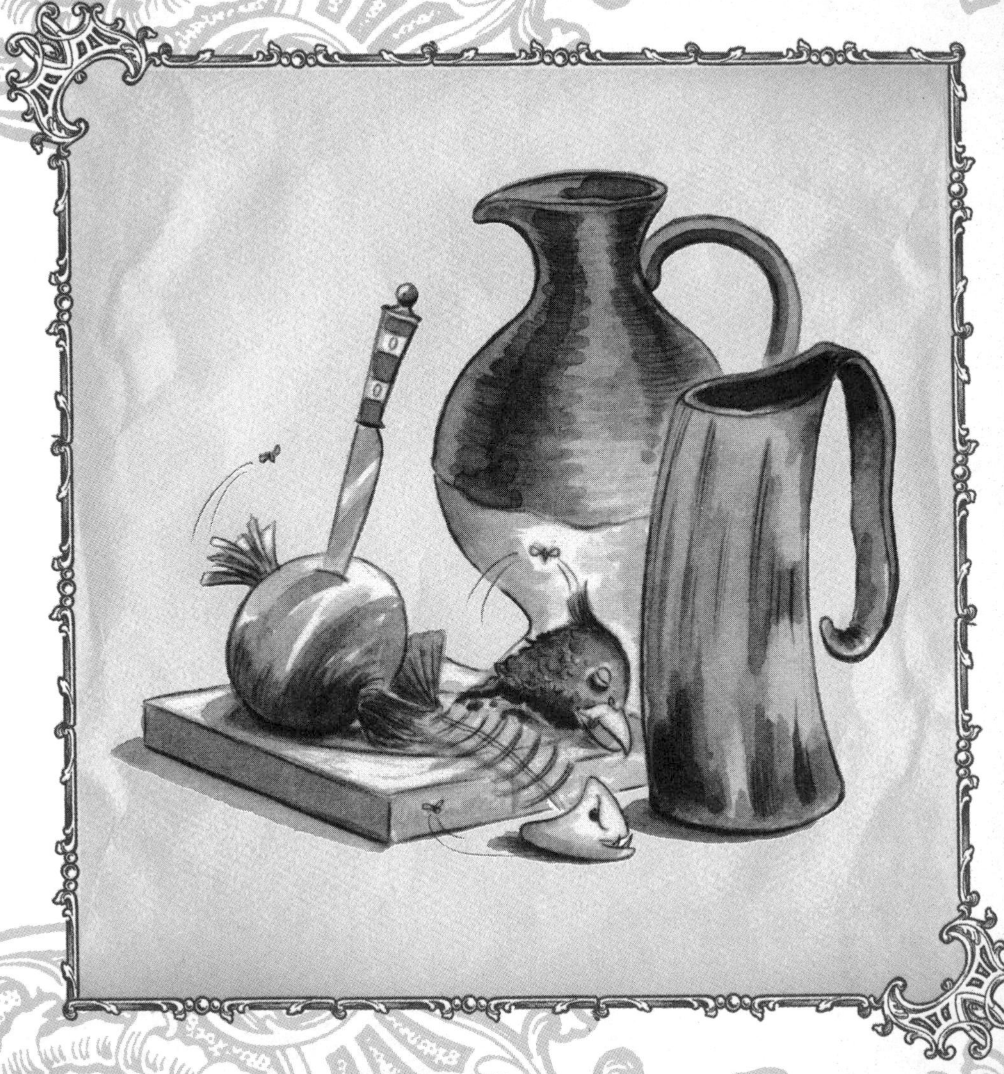

On Food and Drink

I've heard the food in hell is wretched.

—*A Dance with Dragons*

I am not fond of eating horse.
Particularly *my* horse.

—*A Game of Thrones*

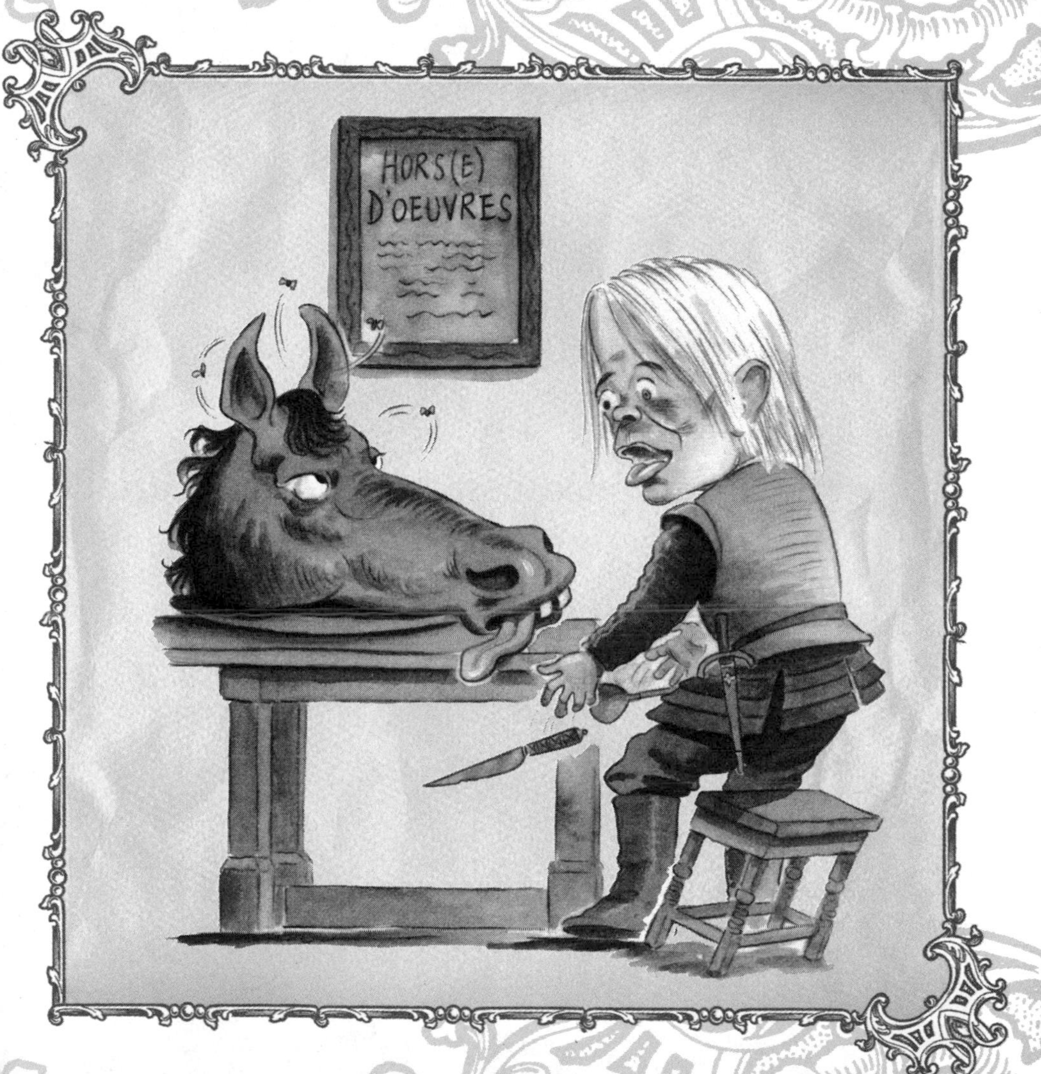
HORS(E) D'OEUVRES

Being randy is the next best thing to being drunk.

—*A Dance with Dragons*

Do I really want to spend the rest of my life eating salt beef and porridge with murderers and thieves?

—*A Dance with Dragons*

Someone should tell the cooks that turnip isn't a meat.

—A Game of Thrones

If I drink enough fire wine
perhaps I'll dream of dragons.

—*A Dance with Dragons*

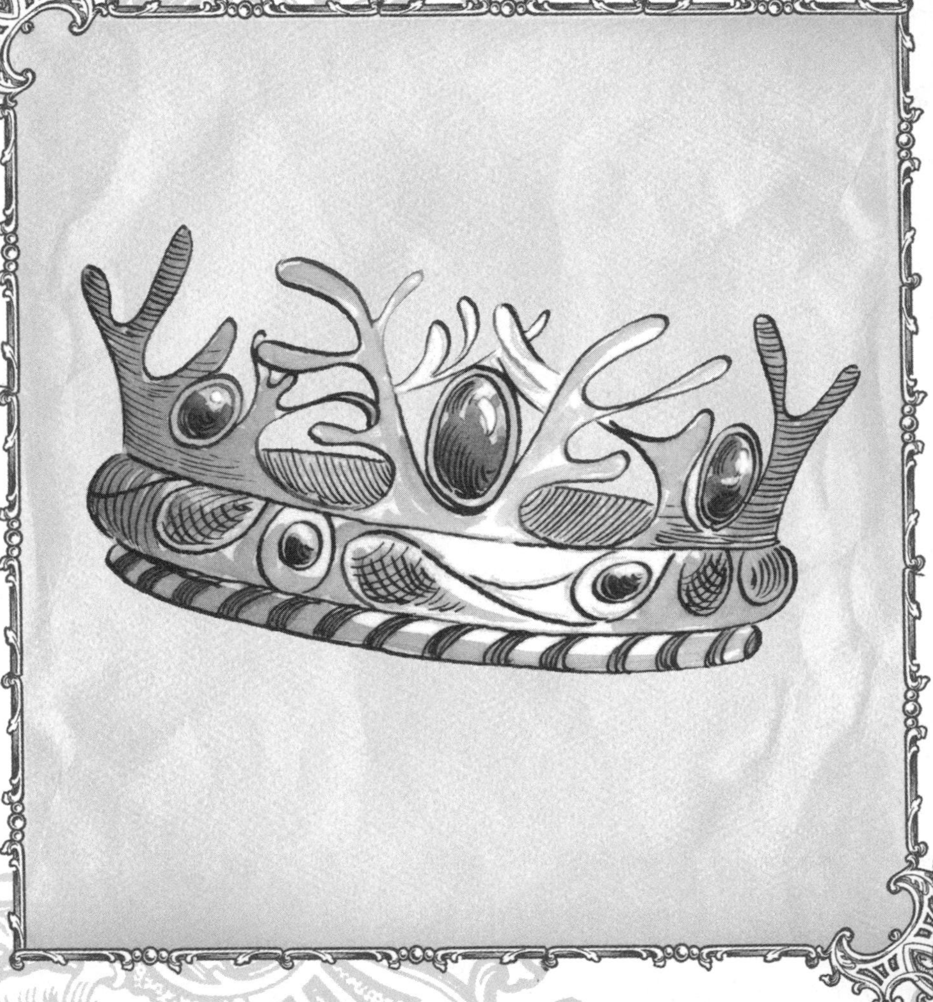

On Kingship

All sorts of people are calling themselves
kings these days.

—*A Clash of Kings*

My nephew is not fit to sit a privy,
let alone the Iron Throne.

—*A Clash of Kings*

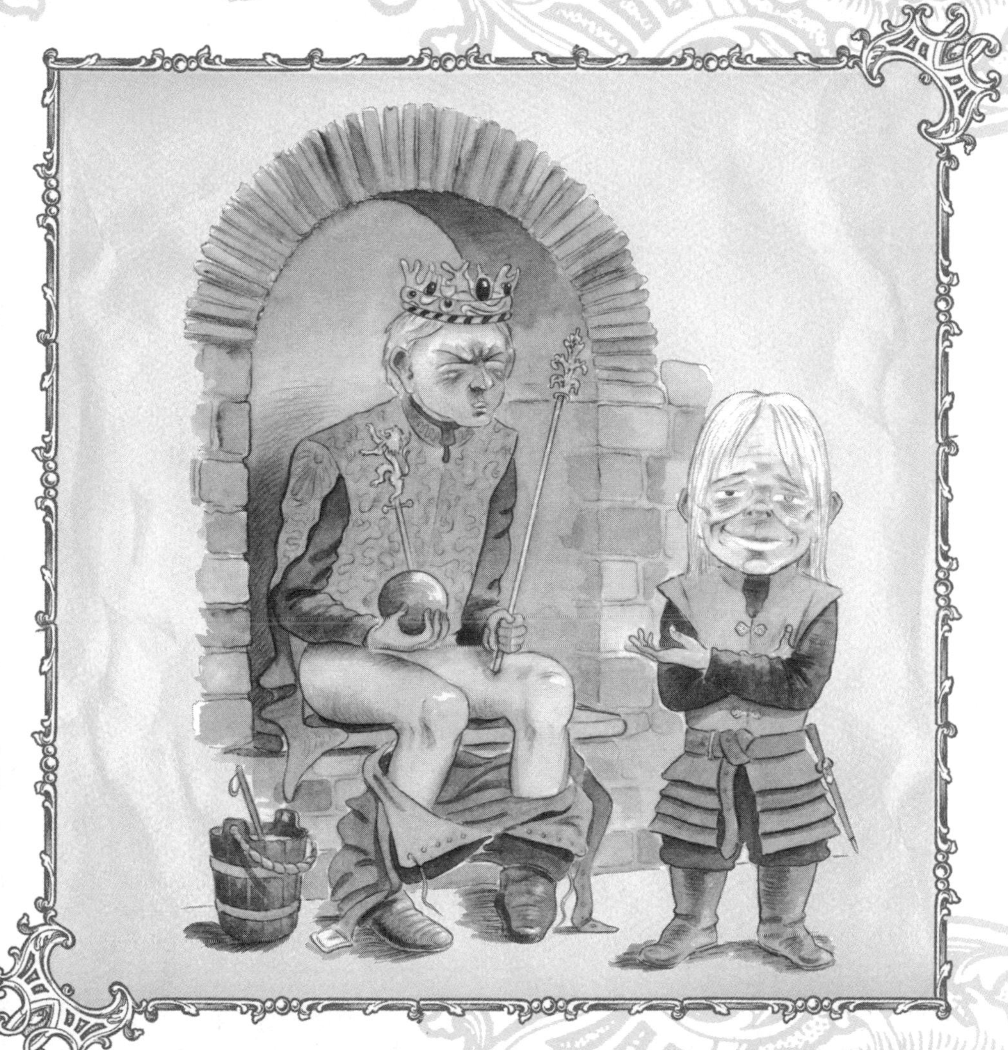

Crowns do queer things to the heads
beneath them.

—A Clash of Kings

Kings are falling like leaves this autumn.

—*A Storm of Swords*

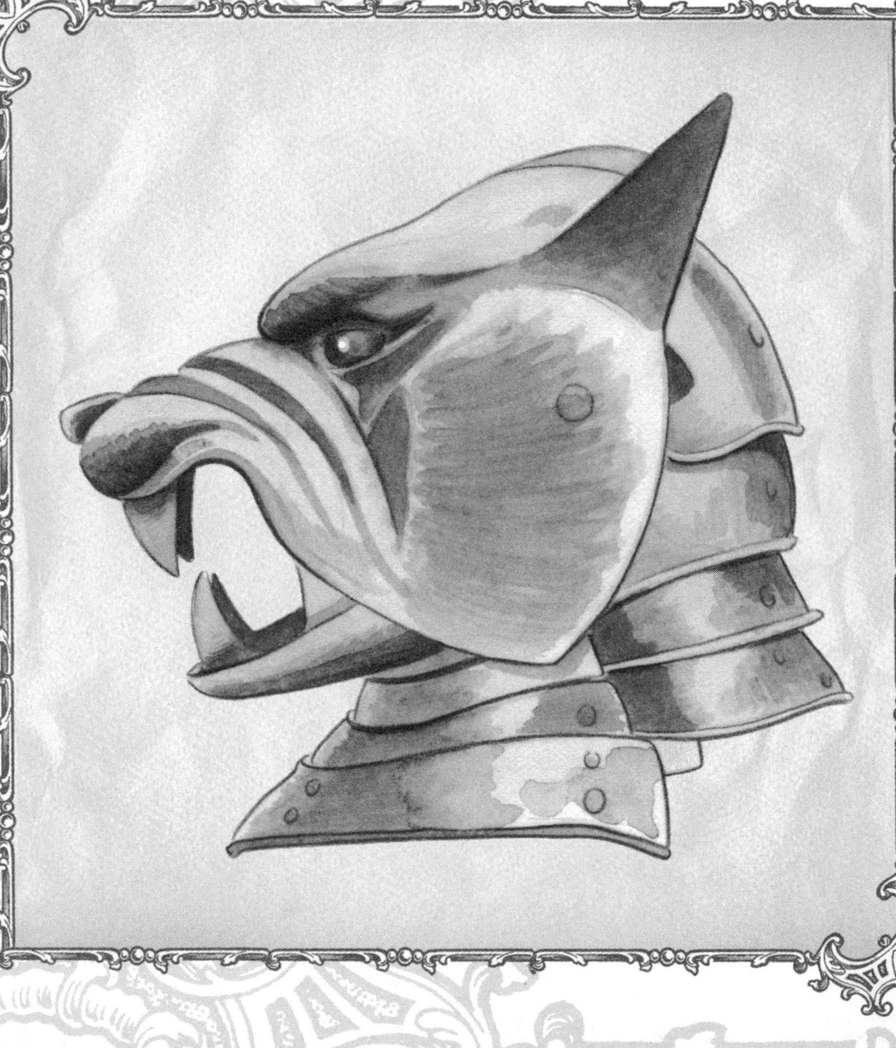

On Realpolitik

Some allies are more dangerous than enemies.

—*A Dance with Dragons*

You can buy a man with gold, but only blood and steel will keep him true.

—*A Dance with Dragons*

Schemes are like fruit,
they require a certain ripening.

—*A Clash of Kings*

It all goes back and back, to our mothers and fathers and theirs before them. We are puppets dancing on the strings of those who came before us, and one day our own children will take up our strings and dance in our steads.

—*A Storm of Swords*

Rebellion makes for queer bedfellows.

—*A Dance with Dragons*

When winter comes, the realm will starve.

—*A Dance with Dragons*

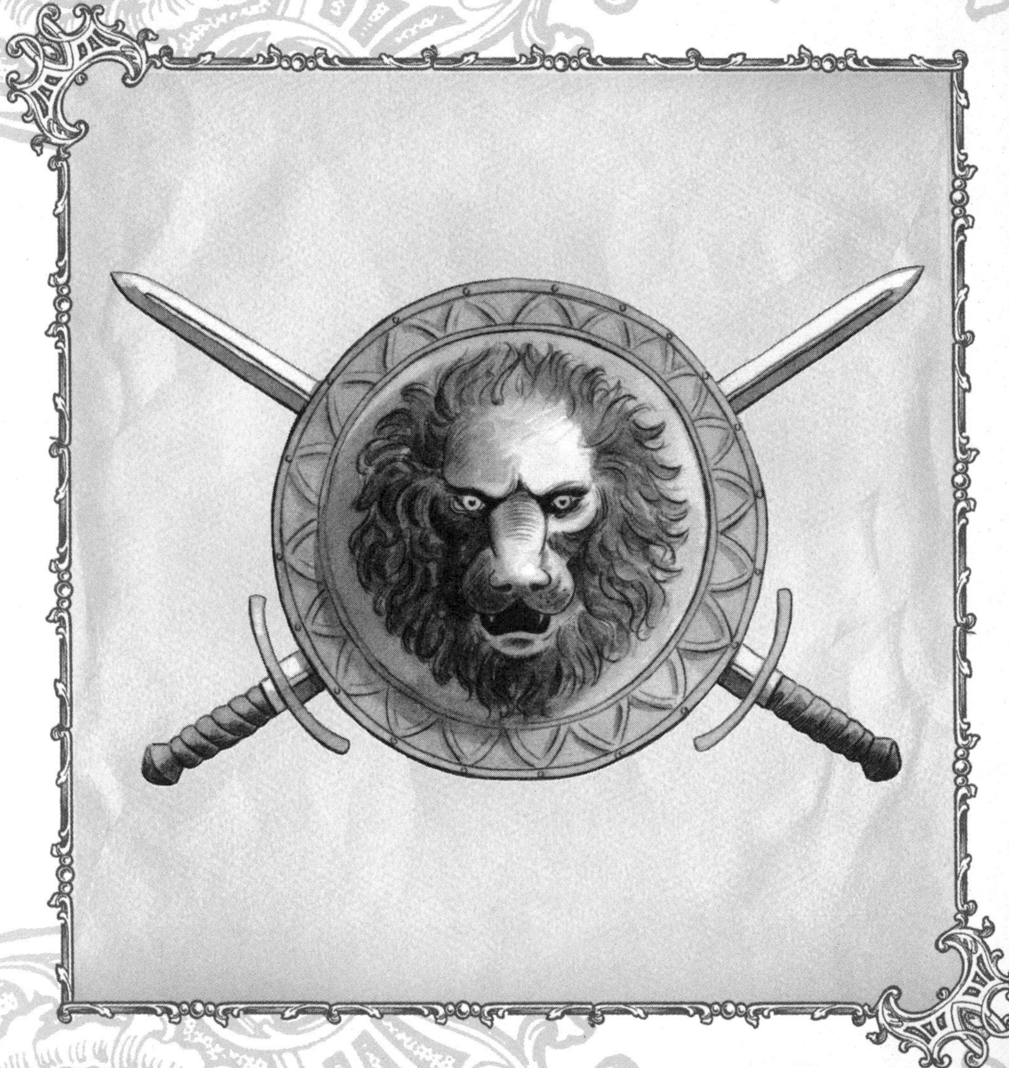

The Art of War

Gold has its uses, but wars are won with iron.

—*A Dance with Dragons*

I sit a chair better than a horse, and I'd sooner hold a wine goblet than a battle-axe. All that about the thunder of the drums, sunlight flashing on armor, magnificent destriers snorting and prancing? Well, the drums gave me headaches, the sunlight flashing on my armor cooked me up like a harvest day goose, and those magnificent destriers shit everywhere.

—*A Clash of Kings*

How many Dornishmen does it take
to start a war? Only one.

—*A Storm of Swords*

Knights know only one way to solve a problem. They couch their lances and charge. A dwarf has a different way of looking at the world.

—*A Dance with Dragons*

He's going to be as useful as nipples
on a breastplate.

—*A Dance with Dragons*

If a man paints a target on his chest, he should expect that sooner or later someone will loose an arrow at him.

—*A Game of Thrones*

A sword through the bowels.
A sure cure for constipation.

—*A Dance with Dragons*

Men fight more fiercely for a king who shares their peril than one who hides behind his mother's skirts.

—*A Clash of Kings*

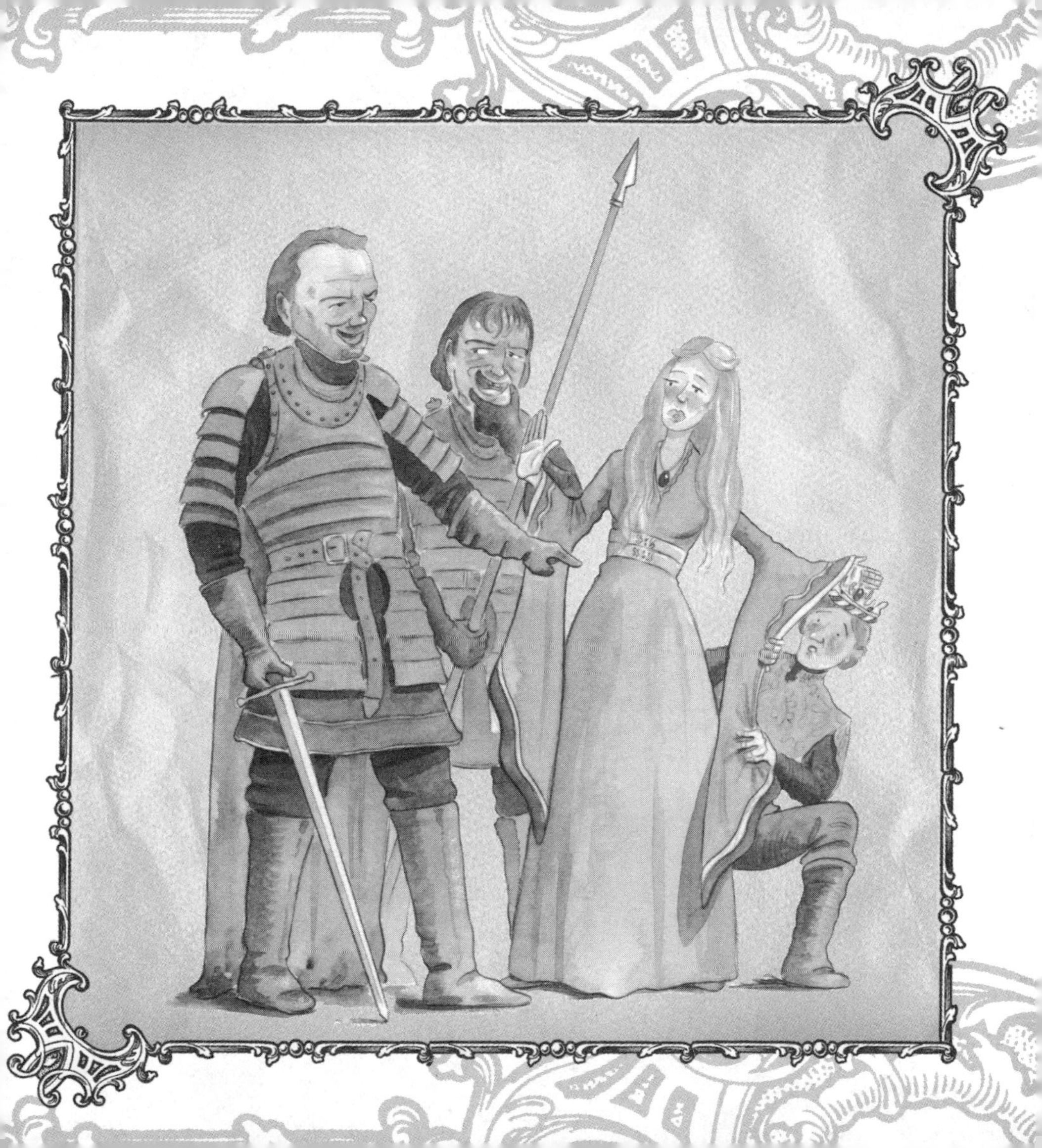

That was the way of war. The smallfolk were slaughtered, while highborn were held for ransom. *Remind me to thank the gods that I was born a Lannister.*

—*A Clash of Kings*

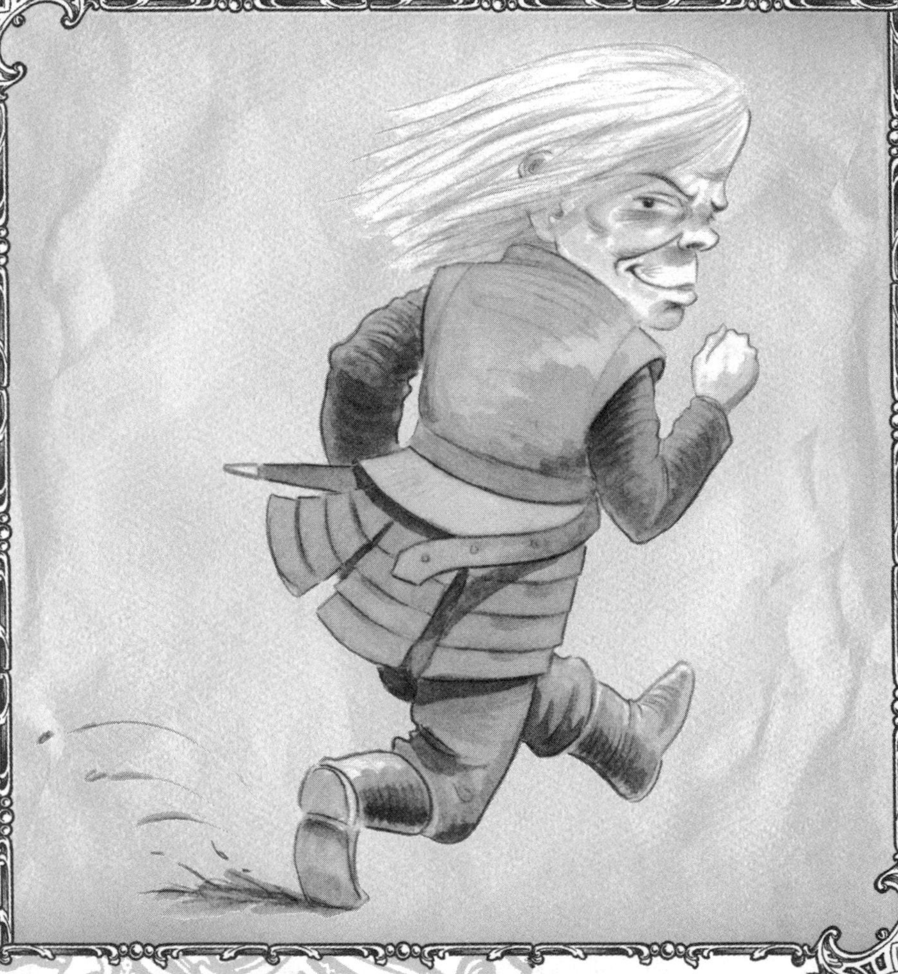

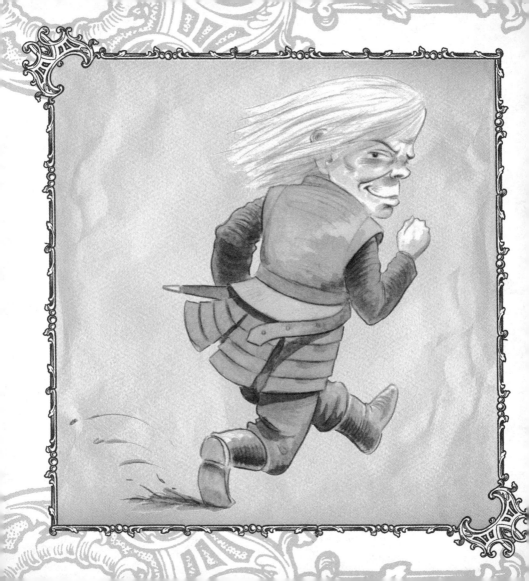

The Art of
Saving Your Skin

Courage and folly are cousins,
or so I've heard.

—*A Clash of Kings*

I'm terrified of my enemies,
so I kill them all.

—*A Clash of Kings*

All this mistrust will sour your stomach and keep you awake at night, 'tis true, but better that than the long sleep that does not end.

—*A Dance with Dragons*

I decline to deliver any message
that might get me killed.

—*A Game of Thrones*

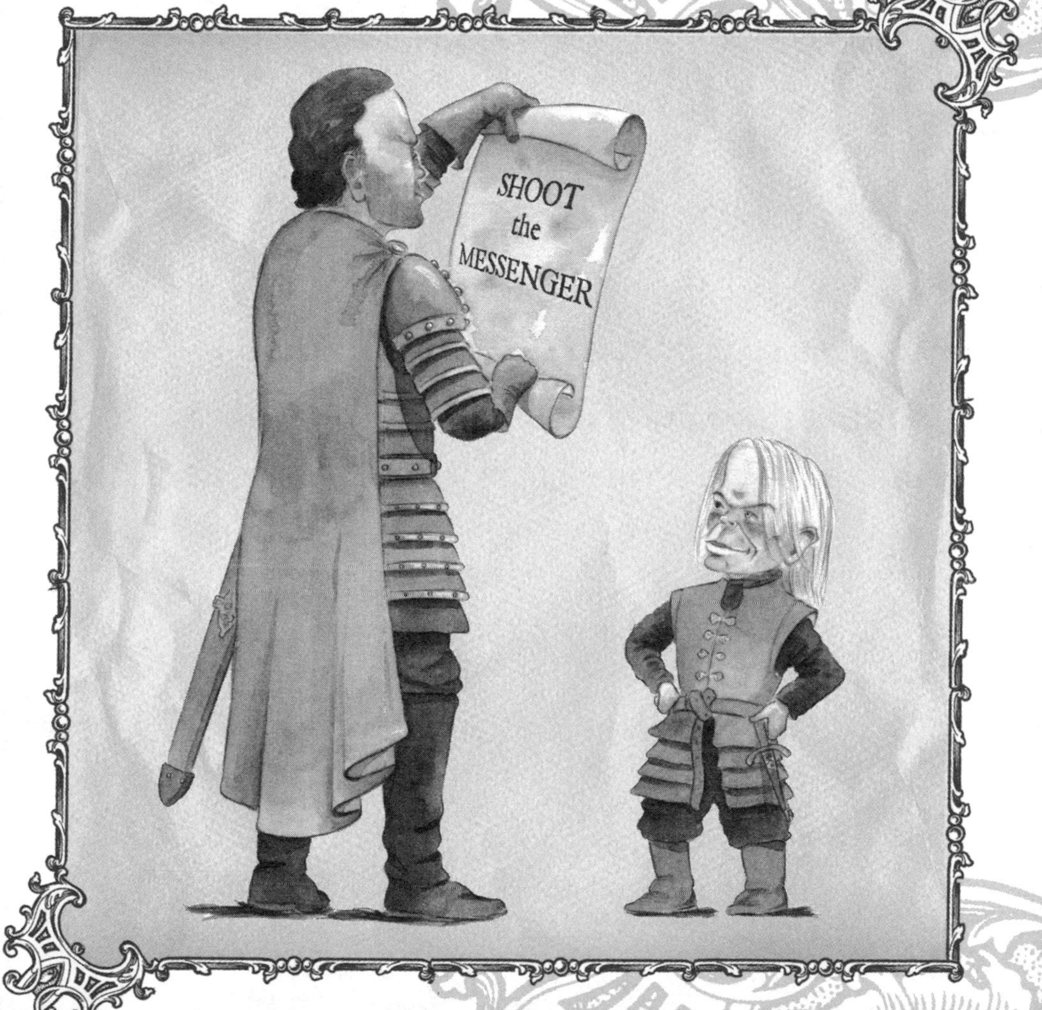
SHOOT
the
MESSENGER

Riding hard and fast by night is a sure way to tumble down a mountain and crack your skull.

—*A Game of Thrones*

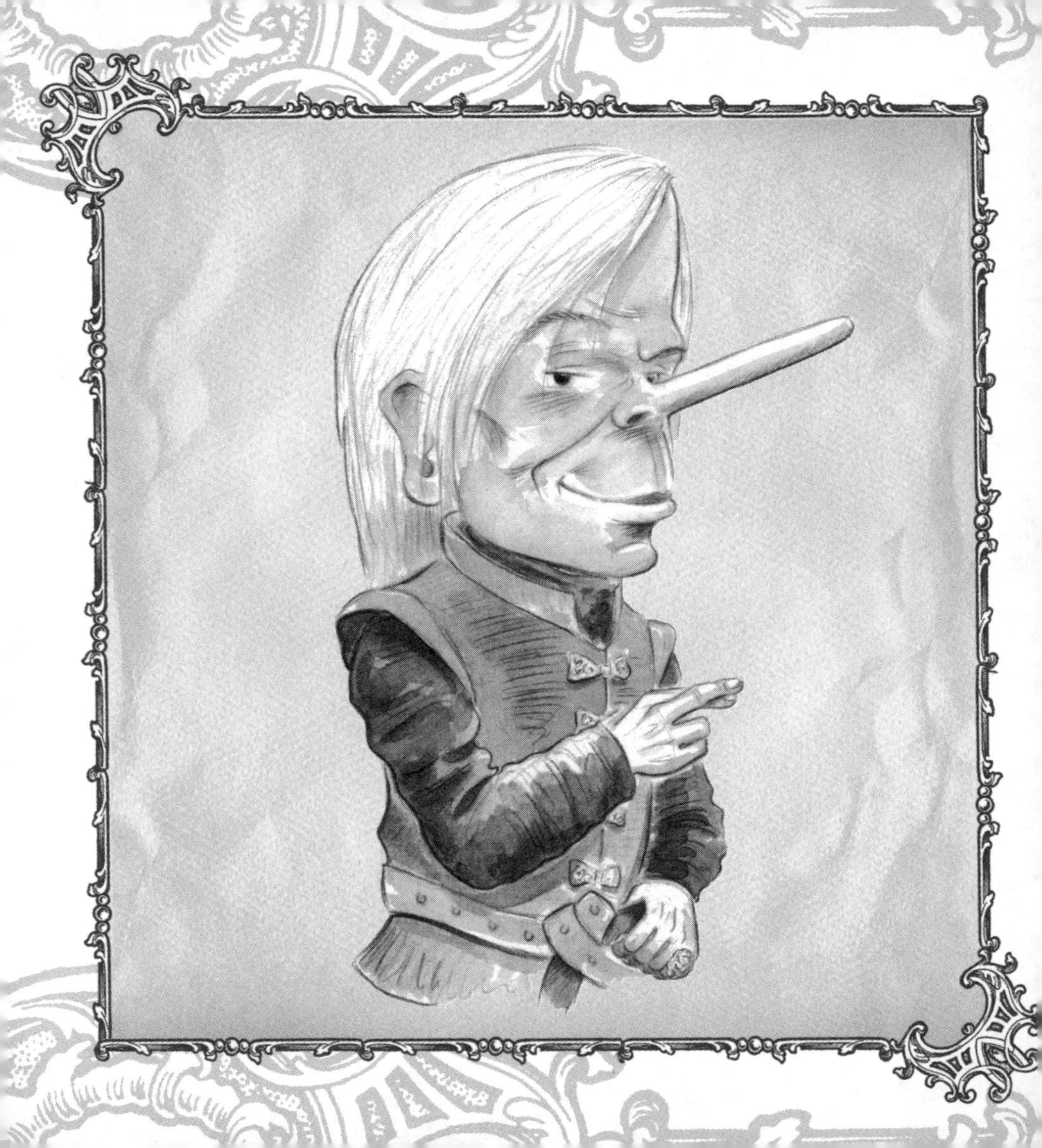

The Art of Lying

Give me sweet lies,
and keep your bitter truths.

—*A Storm of Swords*

How did I lose my nose? I shoved it up your wife's cunt and she bit it off.

—*A Dance with Dragons*

Half-truths are worth more than outright lies.

—*A Storm of Swords*

My father threw me down a well the day
I was born, but I was so ugly that the water
witch who lived down there spat me back.

—*A Dance with Dragons*

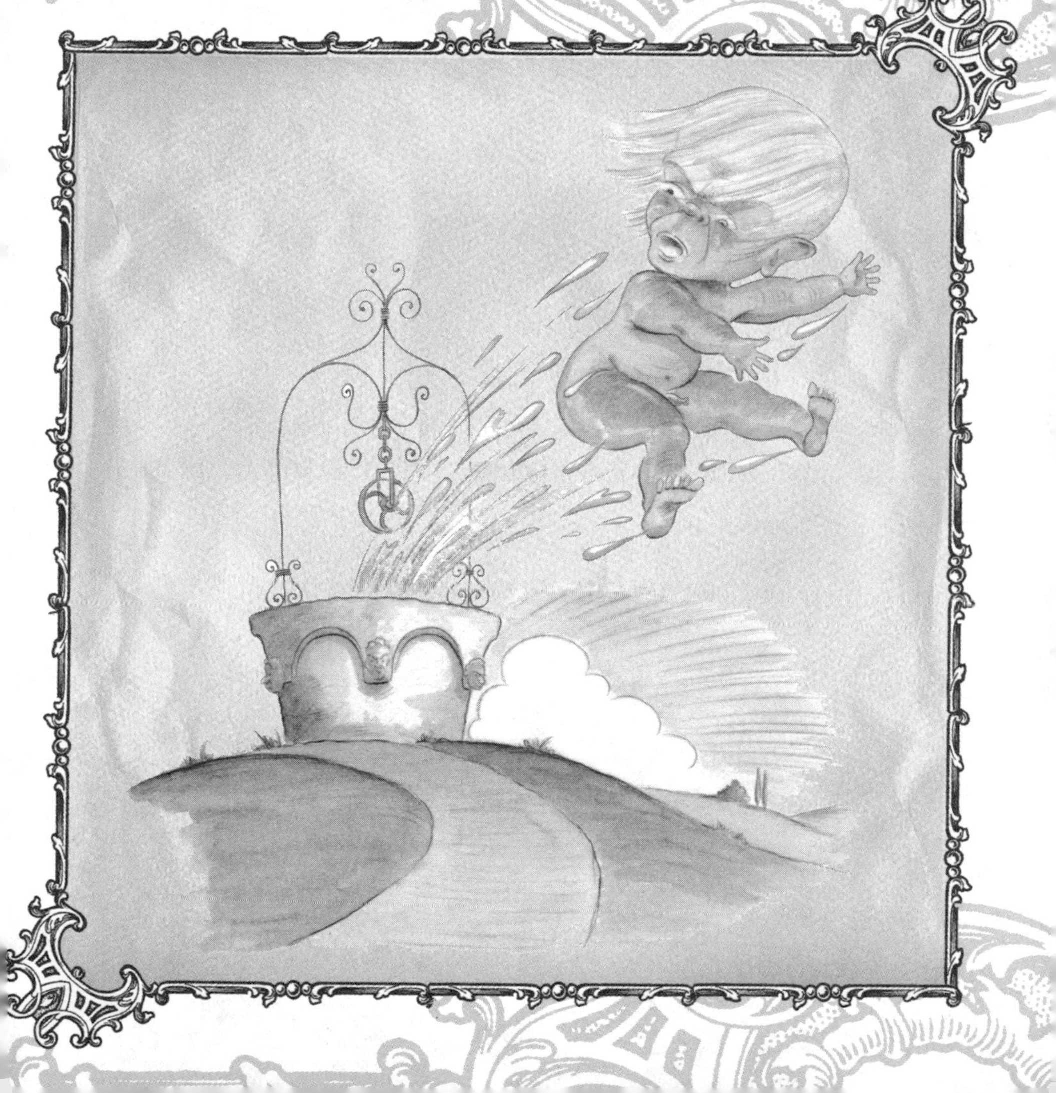

The best lies are seasoned with a bit of truth.

—*A Dance with Dragons*

My mother loved me best of all her children because I was so small. She nursed me at her breast till I was seven. That made my brothers jealous, so they stuffed me in a sack and sold me to a mummer's troupe. When I tried to run off the master mummer cut off half my nose, so I had no choice but to go with them and learn to be amusing.

—*A Dance with Dragons*

The sow I ride is actually my sister. We have the same nose, could you tell? A wizard cast a spell on her, but if you give her a big wet kiss, she'll turn into a beautiful woman. The pity is, once you get to know her, you'll want to kiss her again to turn her back.

—*A Dance with Dragons*

Every touch a lie. I have paid her so much false coin that she half thinks she's rich.

—*A Dance with Dragons*

You'd be astonished at what a boy can make
of a few lies, fifty pieces of silver,
and a drunken septon.

—*A Game of Thrones*

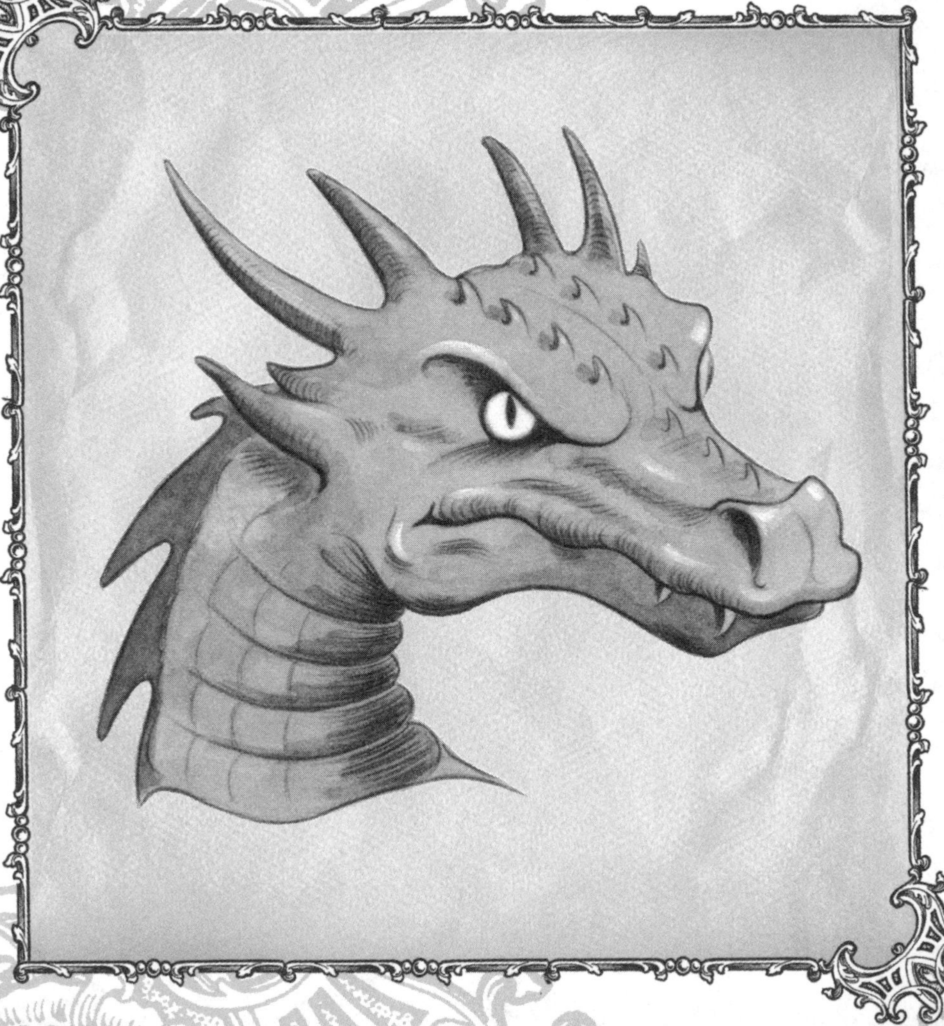

On Dragons
and Other Myths

I believe in steel swords, gold coins, and men's wits. And I believe there once were dragons.

—*A Clash of Kings*

What if we should find that this talk of dragons
was just some sailor's drunken fancy?
This wide world is full of such mad tales.
Grumkins and snarks, ghosts and ghouls,
mermaids, rock goblins, winged horses,
winged pigs, winged lions.

—*A Dance with Dragons*

Next you will be offering me a suit of magic
armor and a palace in Valyria.

—*A Dance with Dragons*

Even a stunted, twisted, ugly little boy can
look down over the world when he's seated
on a dragon's back.

—*A Game of Thrones*

Once a man has seen a dragon in flight, let him stay home and tend his garden in content, for this wide world has no greater wonder.

—*A Dance with Dragons*

If you want to conquer the world,
you best have dragons.

—*A Dance with Dragons*

The Shrouded Lord is just a legend,
no more real than the ghost of Lann the Clever
that some claim haunts Casterley Rock.

—*A Dance with Dragons*

Trust no one. And keep your dragon close.

—*A Dance with Dragons*

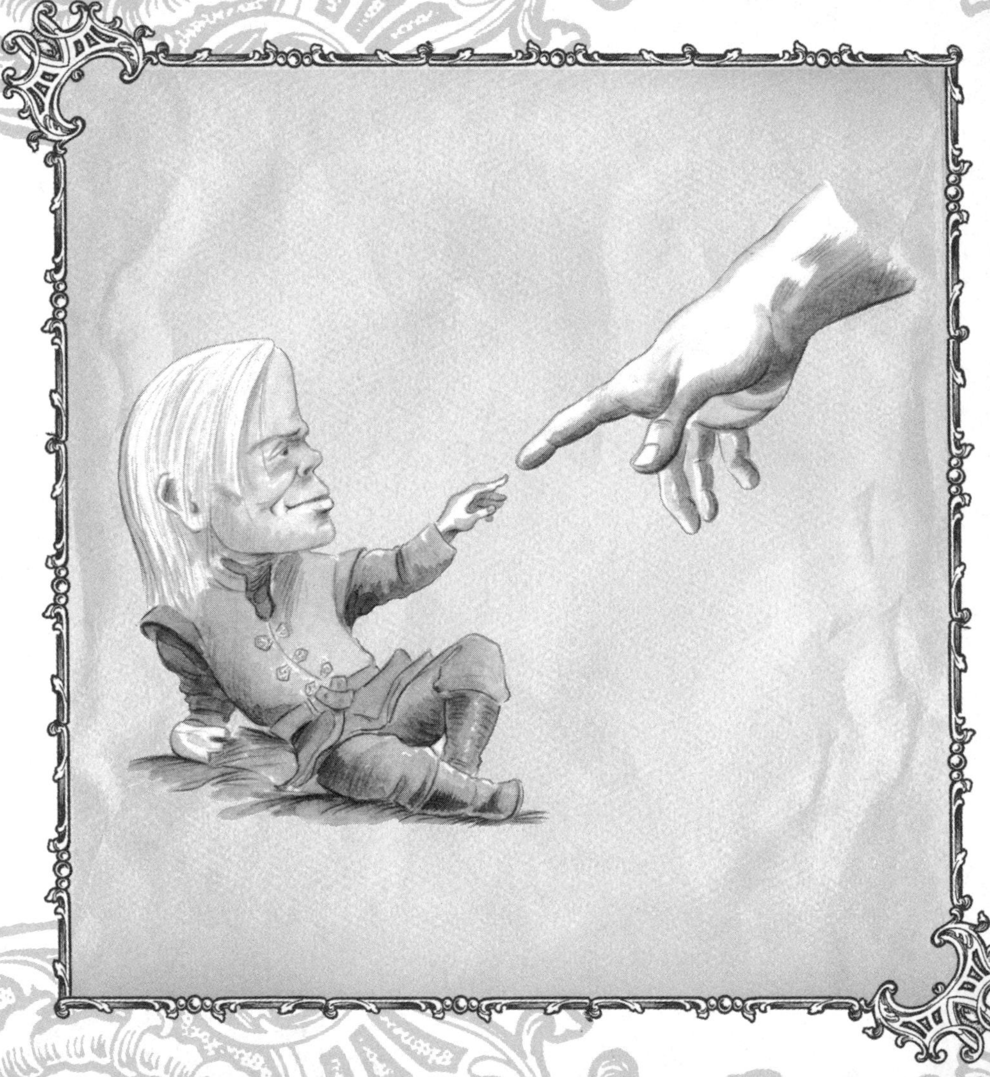

On Religion

What sort of gods make rats and plagues and dwarfs?

—*A Dance with Dragons*

When I was a boy, my wet nurse told me that one day, if men were good, the gods would give the world a summer without ending.

—*A Game of Thrones*

Light our fire and protect us from the dark, blah blah, light our way and keep us toasty warm, the night is dark and full of terrors, save us from the scary things, and blah blah blah some more.

—*A Dance with Dragons*

Somewhere some god is laughing.

—*A Dance with Dragons*

If there are gods to listen, they are monstrous
gods, who torment us for their sport.
Who else would make a world like this,
so full of bondage, blood, and pain?

—*A Dance with Dragons*

The gods give with one hand
and take with the other.

—*A Clash of Kings*

If I could pray with my cock,
I would be much more religious.

—*A Clash of Kings*

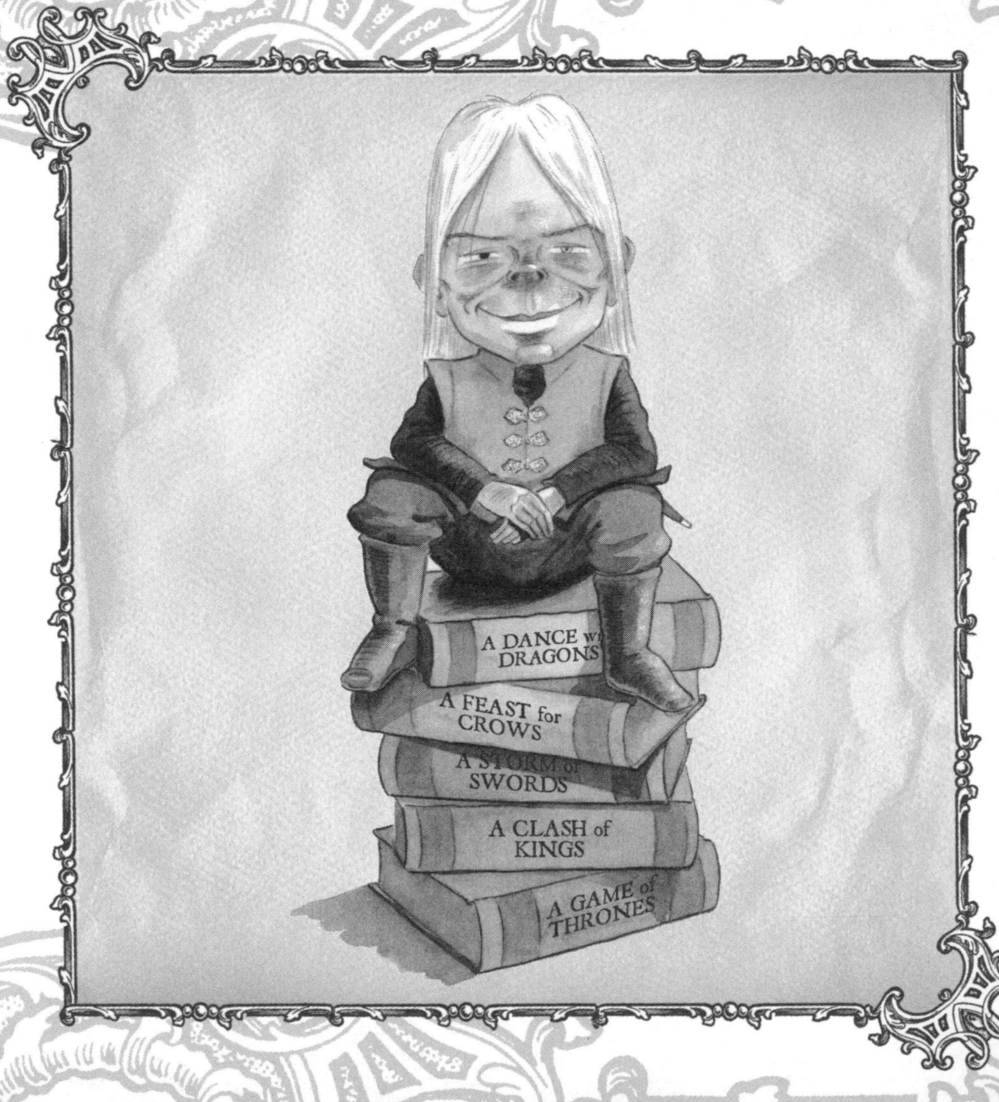
A DANCE
DRAGONS
A FEAST for CROWS
A STORM of SWORDS
A CLASH of KINGS
A GAME of THRONES

About the author

GEORGE R. R. MARTIN is the #1 *New York Times* bestselling author of many novels, including the acclaimed series A Song of Ice and Fire—*A Game of Thrones, A Clash of Kings, A Storm of Swords, A Feast for Crows,* and *A Dance with Dragons.* As a writer-producer, he has worked on *The Twilight Zone, Beauty and the Beast,* and various feature films and pilots that were never made. He lives with the lovely Parris in Santa Fe, New Mexico.

www.georgerrmartin.com